THE TRANSYLVANIAN
INCIDENT

TERRANCE DICKS

The
TRANSYLVANIAN
Incident

Piccadilly Press • London

The rights of Terrance Dicks and Andrew Skilleter to be
identified as Author and Cover illustrator of this work have
been asserted by them in accordance with the
Copyright, Designs and Patents Act 1988

Phototypeset from author's disk by Piccadilly Press.
Printed and bound by Creative Print and Design (Wales),
Ebbw Vale, for the publishers Piccadilly Press Ltd.,
5 Castle Road, London NW1 8PR

A catalogue record for this book is available from
the British Library

ISBNs: 1 85340 474 8 (trade paperback)

3 5 7 9 10 8 6 4 2

Terrance Dicks lives in North London. He has written many books
for Piccadilly Press including the CHANGING UNIVERSE series, the
HARVEY series, THE GOOD, THE BAD AND THE GHASTLY series and
the SECOND SIGHT series.

Cover design by Judith Robertson

PROLOGUE

It was, thought the village policeman, a hell of a night.

He poked the iron stove that stood in the centre of the little room. With its whitewashed stone walls, heavy wooden table and rickety chairs the police station was a simple enough place – and it was a lot better than the dark and stormy night outside, with its icy howling wind.

He ate the last of his sausage, swigged the last of the rough red wine and looked at the Russian-made steel watch on his wrist.

Midnight, time for his last patrol. After that, thank goodness, he could bundle himself up in his blankets and sleep till dawn.

Wrapping himself in his heavy overcoat, and pulling down his cap, he went out into the darkness. As soon as he stepped out of the doorway he was buffeted by the icy wind that raced down from the mountains.

The little police station stood at the bottom of the main village street. Bracing himself, the policeman began the ascent to the main square at the top. If the village inn hadn't locked its doors yet, he might be able to cadge another glass of wine.

Head down against the wind, he began the long, steep climb. There was a full moon, and the cobbled street was bathed in its eerie light. Occasionally, black storm clouds passed across the moon, and there was a moment or two of pitch-black darkness, until the clouds passed over and the moonlight returned.

It was in one of these intervals of darkness that the policeman heard the choking scream.

It came from one of the narrow sidestreets, the ones on his right that ran down towards the river.

The policeman hesitated, tempted to ignore the sound. Perhaps mountain bandits had come down to rob some unfortunate shopkeeper, it happened sometimes. Ferocious, murderous types, these bandits. Armed to the teeth, they travelled in packs like wolves and had no respect for the forces of the law.

Safer not to hear anything.

On the other hand, the district police commandant was even more terrifying than the bandits.

If the commandant heard that some crime had been committed on the constable's patrol, and he'd heard nothing, done nothing . . .

Fumbling to get his heavy revolver from its holster, the policeman set off down the narrow sidestreet.

'Who's there?' he shouted in a quavering voice. 'Stay where you are; this is the police!'

The only answer was a low, blood-curdling growl.

'Halt!' screamed the policeman.

Suddenly the moonlight returned, illuminating a horrifying scene.

A sprawled shape lay on the cobbles some way ahead of him. Crouched over it was another shape, black-cloaked, its head buried in its victim's neck in a ghastly embrace.

The constable's blood turned to ice as age-old terror flooded through him.

'*Strigoi*!' he whispered.

His finger tightened on the trigger in pure

terror, and the shot sounded incredibly loud in the heavy silence, its echoes reverberating around the ancient buildings.

The crouching form raised a white face, its lips bedabbled with blood. It sprang to its feet, the policeman fired again – and there was darkness as the moon vanished behind black clouds.

The darkness lasted only a few seconds, but when the moonlight returned the crouching shape was gone.

The sprawled shape on the cobbles remained.

Resisting the impulse to flee, the policeman stumbled towards the body. It lay face upwards in the moonlight, horn-rimmed glasses askew on the white face, one of the lenses smashed. There was a bloody wound in the neck, just under the jawline.

The dead man wore a tweed suit and an overcoat, well-cut clothes quite unlike those of the local peasants. To his horror the policeman recognised him. He was a foreigner, the solitary tourist staying at the village inn.

This means trouble, big trouble, thought the terrified policeman. The death of a villager, especially from such a cause, might be hushed up without too much fuss. But a foreigner . . .

Suddenly the darkness returned.

Something flapped out of the blackness, hitting the policeman in the face. Claws raked across his cheek and then the thing disappeared into the night with a whirring of leathery wings.

The constable's shaky nerve broke and he turned and fled.

Lights began to go on here and there in the village street – but no one ventured out into the night . . .

Chapter One

HORROR STORY

In the sinister old castle, the final struggle between good and evil reached a terrifying climax.

Vampire hunter Van Helsing chased the black-cloaked Count Dracula up a great marble staircase. Finally he cornered him in the castle hall.

Dracula was just about to disappear down a trapdoor when Van Helsing dashed over.

Dropping the trapdoor lid, Dracula snatched up a handy candlestick and threw it at Van Helsing's head.

Missed!

Dracula hurled himself upon Van Helsing. They grappled . . .

Slowly but surely the Count used his supernatural strength to choke Van Helsing into unconsciousness.

The vampire hunter slumped back. Dracula

hovered above his victim's exposed throat.

In the nick of time Van Helsing recovered . . . Springing to his feet, he threw Dracula off.

For a moment the two circled each other warily.

Then Van Helsing noticed the long curtains covering the big window at the end of the hall. Was that a chink of light between them?

Bounding on to the long wooden table, Van Helsing sprinted along its entire length and took a flying leap at the curtains, ripping them down from the window with his own weight.

A wide shaft of dawn sunlight flooded into the hall.

Van Helsing snatched up a pair of candlesticks, crossing one with the other. With the improvised crucifix he drove Dracula back into the shaft of sunlight – and the vampire count crumbled into dust . . .

The music swelled to a climax and the final credits rolled. I yawned and stretched in my armchair, thinking that Christopher Lee was by far the best screen Dracula.

I thought how young Peter Cushing – Van

Helsing – looked – but then, the film had been made a good forty years ago. The first, and to my mind still the best, of the old Hammer Horror Dracula movies, it had just had its ten millionth showing on late-night TV.

I thought too that it was a hard life being one of the un-dead. So much to remember . . .

Being sure to be tucked up safely in your coffin, filled with the soil of your native Transylvania, well before dawn.

Steering clear of crucifixes, sunlight and running water.

Never ordering the pizza with the garlic topping . . .

And I thought how well the vampire myth – if it was a myth – had lasted. It had started off way back in the murky Middle Ages, and Bram Stoker's book had given it a huge boost, back in eighteen ninety something. Since then there had been hundreds, maybe thousands of books and films about vampires.

Like Dracula himself, who had returned for many a movie sequel, the legend of the vampire refused to die . . .

The door behind me opened suddenly and I

swung round. A tall, black-clad figure stood in the doorway. The light from the TV screen glinted evilly on a high, bald forehead and the lenses of big horn-rimmed spectacles.

It gave me quite a start – until I realised it wasn't Count Dracula back from the dead but Dad, back from one of his endless scientific conventions.

I'm Matt Stirling, by the way. Dad – Professor James Stirling, to give him his full title – and I together make up the Scientific Research Institute's Department of Paranormal Studies.

Dad's a top space scientist and all-round egghead. He agreed to take the paranormal studies job, much against his will, when his space research grant ran out. The fact that the new job carried a large salary and unlimited expenses helped to persuade him.

At the same time he had to take responsibility for me. Dad and Mum had split up when I was still a baby. He went off to America and she brought me up on her own. When she died in a road accident her sister Ellen took over. When Ellen's husband retired and they both went to live in Spain, Dad suddenly found himself holding the baby again. Only by this time the baby had grown up into a six-foot fifteen-year-old – me!

Since he got landed with me and the para-normal studies job more or less together, Dad decided to merge his two problems. He took me out of school, took charge of my education himself and made me his personal assistant and general dogsbody. The arrangement hadn't worked out too badly – so far. Dad and I are slowly getting used to each other after a fifteen-year interval. It hasn't been easy.

Mind you, we agree on some things. For instance, we agree that one of us is arrogant, obstinate and intolerant, lacks proper respect for authority and consideration for the rights of others and has far too high an opinion of himself and his own abilities.

We just disagree about which one of us it is.

Dad took off his black raincoat and flung it over a chair. I'm still trying to train him to be tidy.

'What rubbish are you wasting your time with now?' he asked, tactful as ever.

I switched off the TV. 'The old Hammer *Dracula*,' I said. 'Widely recognised as a classic. You're just not into popular culture.'

'You'll give yourself nightmares again.'

That was below the belt. I had had nightmares recently, but they hadn't been caused by anything as harmless as old horror movies. They were connected with some very strange events we'd been investigating at Borley Rectory, once known as the most haunted house in England.

To change the subject I said, 'How was the conference? "The Future of Space Travel", wasn't it? How does it look?'

'Bleak,' said Dad grimly. 'This government is no keener on spending money on really important things than the last one.'

Dad tends to be single-minded about his pet subject. As far as he's concerned the government ought to close down all the schools and hospitals, cut off all social benefits, cancel the Millenium Dome, and spend all the money on a really decent Mars rocket – designed by him!

Not wanting to get him started I asked, 'See anyone you know?'

'Just the usual deadheads.'

Dad doesn't think too highly of his scientific colleagues.

'Oh, and Ms Alexander was there,' he added.

'Talking on the security aspects of space research.'

'Well, she's no deadhead,' I said.

Ms Alexander was Director of a mysterious security agency. We'd worked together on the Borley Rectory business, and on a previous affair at Stonehenge.

'She's asked us to call in and see her tomorrow morning,' Dad went on. 'Something has cropped up apparently, a request for help from some overseas security agency. It could mean a trip abroad.'

'Did she say which security agency?' I asked.

'Eastern Europe. Romania.'

'Weird!'

'Times are changing, Matthew. International co-operation is the rule these days. Ms Alexander was telling me that she often works quite closely with the KGB. Furthermore . . .'

'That's not what I meant,' I said, cutting off the coming lecture on international relations. 'What's weird is that I was watching a vampire movie and now you tell me we may be going to Romania.'

'What's strange about that?'

'If I remember my basic geography, Romania

includes a province called Transylvania – the traditional home of the vampire!'

'My dear Matthew,' said Dad scornfully. 'There could be all kinds of reasons why an Eastern European security agency asks for help from their British colleagues. I very much doubt if it's got anything to do with vampires!'

As it happened, that was just where he was wrong . . .

'I couldn't make up my mind whether to ask for your help or not, Professor Stirling,' said Ms Alexander the next morning. 'It's such a . . . bizarre affair. Then seeing you at the conference, I thought, why not?'

We were in a small but luxurious conference room in an anonymous tower-block beside the Thames. On the other side of the highly polished table sat Ms Alexander, as neat, precise and efficient-looking as ever. Beside her was her new deputy director, a large and cheerful young man called James Wainwright.

I was glad they'd promoted Jim Wainwright. He'd been a great help to us in the past and was a great improvement on her previous deputy, an acid-tongued bureaucrat called Harker, who'd come to a sticky end over the Borley Rectory business.

'Of course, if I can help . . .' said Dad formally.

For once Ms Alexander seemed strangely diffident. 'It's certainly not in our line, but it might possibly be in yours . . .'

'Perhaps if you could tell me what it's all about,' said Dad. I could see he was getting impatient, he hates dithering.

Ms Alexander still didn't seem able to get to the point. 'Are you familiar with the current situation in Romania, Professor Stirling?'

'Reasonably so,' snapped Dad. He hates to admit he's not an expert on absolutely everything.

'Like many Eastern European countries they've cast off Communist rule. These days Romania calls itself a presidential democracy.'

'Very admirable, I'm sure,' Dad returned impatiently. 'But I fail to see how it concerns . . .'

'Their President's whole policy is based on closer links with the West,' said Ms Alexander. 'He has to present Romania as a modern, progressive country to get the financial aid and the foreign investment they so desperately need.'

'Quite so,' said Dad, by now visibly losing patience. I decided to give things a prod, before he blew up completely.

'So what's stopping the march of democratic progress?' I asked. 'And how does it concern us?'

Ms Alexander drew a deep breath and took the plunge. 'There seems to have been a fresh outbreak of vampirism in Transylvania . . .'

Chapter Two

MURDER

I just couldn't resist it.

I turned to Dad and said triumphantly, 'Aha! I hate to say I told you so – but I told you so!'

Ms Alexander looked baffled. 'I'm sorry?'

'Just another of Matthew's stupid jokes,' said Dad furiously. He got to his feet. 'Ms Alexander, I can scarcely believe you would waste my time and yours with this . . . this utter nonsense. Come along, Matthew!'

I didn't move. Instead I said firmly, 'Hold it, Dad!'

He swung round and gave me his well-known withering glare. I ignored it. I'd been glared at so often that by now I was fireproof.

'I'm sorry if I upset you, but that's not the point. Do you really think Ms Alexander would waste her time as well as ours by sending for us over something pointless and trivial? Why not have the courtesy to listen? If you're still not interested, all you have to do is say no.'

Dad didn't say anything – but he sat down again.

'Thank you, Matthew,' said Ms Alexander. She looked at Dad. 'I suppose I can't really blame you for your reaction, Professor Stirling. I felt much the same way myself when James here first brought me the file.' She turned to Wainwright. 'James?'

Wainwright opened a buff file in front of him. 'I can't guarantee you a vampire, professor, but there's definitely a corpse. A man called Corbie, Doctor Henry Corbie. He was a United Nations financial expert, in Romania on some kind of fact-finding mission. He was found dead in the street in a little mountain village with an unpronounce-able name.'

'What was the cause of death?' I asked.

'Loss of blood. There was a wound in his neck.'

'Two neat little punctures?' I asked.

Wainwright consulted the file. 'Not exactly. His throat had been torn out.'

Dad said, 'Is there any evidence that it wasn't

an animal? A wolf, a wild dog, something like that?'

'There's a pretty extraordinary statement from the local constable,' Wainwright replied. 'He was doing his rounds at around midnight when he heard a strange noise from a sidestreet. He investigated and found a black-cloaked figure crouching over a body. He fired at it, twice, but the bullets had no effect. Then the thing turned into a bat, flew at him and clawed his face, and vanished into the night.'

Dad snorted. 'The man was drunk – or mad.'

'He's pretty nearly mad at the moment,' said Wainwright. 'He's in the local hospital, in a high fever and totally delirious. Some kind of infection from deep scratches on his face . . .'

There was a moment of silence.

Then Ms Alexander said, 'This whole thing is immensely embarrassing for the Romanian government, Professor Stirling. The death of someone in Doctor Corbie's position in such bizarre circumstances . . . The United Nations is pressing for action. My opposite number in Bucharest, Colonel Roman, has turned to me for help and I can scarcely refuse.'

'Why you?' I asked. 'I mean, why the British Security Service?'

'Apparently the colonel's father worked with British secret agents in some kind of anti-Nazi resistance movement during the war. The colonel was brought up to have a very high opinion of Britain and its Secret Service.'

She couldn't have said anything more likely to win Dad over. He's an old-fashioned patriot who still believes British is best. 'It's hard to see what we can do,' he said. 'But if you really think we can help them, we'll certainly try.'

He turned to me. 'You agree, Matthew?'

'Provided we lay in a good supply of garlic, sharp stakes and crucifixes,' I said.

Dad forced a grim smile.

Ms Alexander didn't look too amused either.

'I can't tell you how grateful I am,' she said. 'I agree with you, professor, the whole story is ridiculous. But I've been asked to provide expert help – and in this particular field, you're the only expert I've got. Now if you'll excuse me? James here will make all the necessary travel arrangements . . .'

Ms Alexander went off, probably looking

forward to dealing with some nice normal spies.

Jim Wainwright got cracking on the arrangements. 'We'll just nip down to photography first. We're going to fix you up with special diplomatic papers. Then you'll have to see the doc for some jabs . . . Oh, and I've booked you on the British Airways flight from Gatwick tomorrow morning.'

I gave him a look. 'You were pretty sure we'd go, then?'

'A vampire-hunting trip to sunny Transylvania? How could you resist? I only wish I was coming with you . . . Now, let me give you a quick briefing on the local political situation . . .'

A few hours later we were heading home in a taxi with sore arms and an impressive sheaf of documents.

We also had a copy of Wainwright's file. Dad was speed-reading it as the taxi began the long climb back up to Hampstead.

He closed it with a snap and said, 'I know you must have your little joke, Matthew – but you don't really believe the unfortunate Doctor Corbie was killed by a vampire, do you?'

'I believe that policeman believes he saw a

vampire,' I said. 'Vampire legends must be part of the local culture. If he found a dark shape crouching over a body he probably saw what he was conditioned to see. I imagine the locals think all foreigners must be wealthy. Perhaps the whole thing was just a mugging that went too far.'

Dad sighed. 'That's very much what I thought myself. I imagine we're dealing with some sordid local murderer. And how we're supposed to catch him if the Romanian police can't . . .'

I nodded and glanced at my watch. There was still time to pop out and do a bit of shopping before I packed . . .

About half an hour later I was walking along the busy high street. They'd have garlic at the grocers, but where was I going to find a crucifix?

I caught sight of a tall, white-faced man in a long, dark coat – or was it a cloak? – on the other side of the road. He seemed to be staring fixedly at me.

He was still there when I came out of the shop with my little bag of garlic cloves. Could he be following me?

I decided all this vampire stuff must be getting to me already – and went off to look for a crucifix. After all, there's no point in taking unnecessary chances . . .

It's a long way to Transylvania.

The direct flight to Bucharest takes three hours and twenty minutes. We were travelling first class to preserve our diplomatic cover. This meant high-class snacks for us both and free champagne for Dad, and of course he took full advantage of it. Pretty soon he dozed off. I contented myself with a Coke, took an assortment of books from my hand luggage and sat back to brush up on my vampire lore.

It was a pretty horrifying story, with facts – if they were facts – all mixed up with legend, myth and downright fiction.

A fifteenth-century king called Vlad Tepesh had the unpleasant habit of impaling his enemies on sharpened stakes. Revolting as he undoubtedly was, there's no evidence that he was ever accused of being a vampire. Unfortunately for him, Bram Stoker borrowed one of Vlad's many titles, and gave it to his fictional creation, Count Dracula.

Vlad's been stuck with his bloodsucking reput-
ation ever since.

The first historical vampire figure was
female, a Countess Elizabeth Bathory who lived in
the early seventeenth century. She used to kidnap
local peasant girls, kill them and bathe in their
blood, believing it kept her young and beautiful.
Eventually the king got to hear of her crimes and
ordered that she be bricked up in her own bed-
chamber and left there to die.

Apart from general bloodthirstiness, links
between Vlad and Countess Elizabeth and
vampirism were pretty thin.

But later in the seventeenth century, there
seemed to be a positive epidemic of vampirism.
Village after village reported that the dead were
climbing out of their graves and coming back to
suck the blood of the living.

One typical story tells how the local military
commander had several graves dug up – to find
corpses showing no sign of decay, with fresh
blood on their lips. The bodies were then all
burned to ashes – an even more effective way of
dealing with vampires than the traditional stake
through the heart.

Similar stories persisted in Eastern Europe throughout the seventeenth century, and carried on right up till the twentieth. As late as 1909 a Transylvanian castle was burned down by local peasants, who believed it to be the home of a vampire.

In Western Europe the vampire flourished in fiction. Bram Stoker's novel *Dracula* came out in the 1890s. It was a best-selling book and a smash hit on the stage. Soon after that the silent movies took up the tale with *Nosferatu*. Bela Lugosi played the count in black-and-white films. Then came the Hammer Horror films in glorious blood-red Technicolor – which is where we came in.

Awash with horrors, I put away the books and lay back, brooding over the weird mixture of history, legend and fiction. I had the strangest feeling that there was some basic truth hidden underneath it all, something yet to be discovered . . .

I got another strange feeling as well, that odd sensation you get when someone behind you is staring at you. There's no way you can know that they're staring at you, but somehow you do . . .

The feeling became so strong that I just had

to check up on it. I was in the aisle seat, so I turned round and looked back.

A few rows behind me sat a tall, white-faced man dressed in black. It was the man I'd seen in the high street. He was fixing me with a burning stare. I turned my head back quickly, but it was no use. I still seemed to feel that stare.

I thought about waking Dad, but it would all sound too silly. He'd think I was cracking up.

I considered getting up and going to the toilet, dropping a clove of garlic or a crucifix in the man's lap as I went past. (I'd managed to get hold of a crucifix in the museum shop just off the high street. It was a reproduction of the cross of some saint in a medieval church. I hoped the association would give it a bit of extra holiness.) Unfortunately, I'd left both garlic and cross in my suitcase, now somewhere in the baggage hold. I hadn't expected to need them before I reached Transylvania.

Telling myself I was just being silly, I huddled down in my seat and tried to get some sleep. Eventually I dropped into an uneasy doze – and dreamed of a sinister, black-cloaked figure sweeping towards me through the darkness. I was having my nightmare after all.

A hand on my shoulder jolted me awake, heart pounding and sweat on my forehead. For a moment I thought the vampire had come for me, but it was only Dad.

'Time to wake up, Matthew, we're starting the final descent.'

Once again I considered telling him about the man behind us, but I decided against it. Dad was quite capable of asking him who the devil he was staring at, and I didn't want to risk a row with one of the un-dead just yet. Not till I got my hands on my garlic and crucifix anyway . . .

The plane glided down towards Bucharest, first stop on our journey to Transylvania, traditional home of the vampire. I just wished I could get rid of the uneasy feeling that we were bringing one back with us . . .

Chapter Three

WELCOME TO TRANSYLVANIA

The plane touched down, nervous passengers sighed with relief, and the usual pre-exit scramble began, with people taking hand luggage from the overhead lockers, jamming the aisles and looking impatiently at the plane's exit doors.

When the doors finally opened a burly, heavily-moustached type in a baggy black suit was first on board. He spoke to the chief steward and the steward pointed down the aisle – at us.

I noticed that some of our fellow passengers, presumably returning Romanians, looked nervously at him, and sympathetically at us. I heard someone whisper fearfully, '*Securitate!*'

The Securitate, as I knew from Wainwright's briefing, was the SRI, the Romanian Information Service. In other words, the secret police.

They'd ruled the country with an iron hand

in the bad old days, blackmailing half of the population into informing on the other half. Nowadays they were supposed to be reformed and democratic, like everything else in Romania. But according to Wainwright they were still very much a power in the land, and very much feared.

We gathered up our hand luggage and joined the line shuffling down the aisle. When we reached the door the security man stood waiting for us. Ignoring me, he addressed Dad in a deep, heavily accented voice. 'You are Professor Stirling.' It was a statement, not a question. When Dad nodded he barked, 'Papers!' He held out his hand.

I didn't care for his tone – or his manner either, come to that. It was bored, almost contemptuous, the voice of someone certain he'll be obeyed.

I could see Dad didn't like it much either, but he fished out his diplomatic passport and accompanying documentation and I did the same.

The security man glanced at the documents and handed them back to us. 'You will come with me.' It was another statement, made in the same bored, authoritarian voice.

I said, 'Just a minute.'

He looked at me in utter amazement.

Deliberately mimicking his tone, I said, 'Papers!'

You could hear the gasps of astonishment right down the plane.

'You seem to know us, but we don't know you,' I went on. 'You could be anyone.'

The security man gave me a long hard stare and then transferred it to Dad.

Dad gave me a scorching glare as well, but to his credit the old boy backed me up. 'It seems a perfectly reasonable request. As my son says, we have no idea who you are.'

The security man said, 'I am Sergeant Janos. Securitate!' He seemed to think the dreaded name should be enough, but I was feeling obstinate.

I just stood there, looking at him expectantly. I held out my hand.

After a moment he took a worn black plastic folder from his pocket and handed it over. Apart from the fact that it showed his picture, the identity card meant nothing to me – he could have been from the Romanian Gas Board for all I knew.

Still, I'd made my point.

I studied the folder gravely and then handed

it to Dad. He gave it a brief glance and handed it back. (We'd been holding the queue up all this time but nobody was complaining.)

Janos said, 'Colonel Roman is waiting. He is not a patient man. You will come with me – please.'

This time there was a tinge of desperation in his voice.

Dad said, 'Of course. After you, sergeant.'

We didn't get to see much of Bucharest's Otopeni Airport. Janos led us off the plane and whisked us through customs and immigration formalities at top speed, way ahead of everyone else. Our luggage, he assured us, would be taken straight to our hotel. Colonel Roman wanted to see us at once.

In no time at all we were coming out of the main entrance of the airport where a black limousine stood waiting.

As I was about to get in, I got that burning sensation in the back of my neck again. I turned and saw the black-clad, white-faced man from the plane. He was standing in the airport entrance, fixing us with that same burning stare.

Dad and I got in the back of the limousine, Janos got in front, and we pulled away.

Dad had been quietly seething ever since the scene on the plane. He spoke in a low, angry voice.

'Matthew, we are guests here, and we need the co-operation of the authorities. What possessed you to behave in that fashion?'

'Just making a point,' I said. 'We're not just any old tourists, we're visiting experts. We'll never get anywhere if we let them push us around.'

To be honest I was justifying myself after the event. What I'd said was true enough, but I hadn't thought of it at the time. Janos had got up my nose and I'd reacted instinctively.

To my surprise a deep chuckle came from the front of the car. 'Boy has spirit,' said Sergeant Janos. 'Long time since anyone ask me for my papers!'

Dad gave me a thoughtful look, and fell silent.

The limousine took us through a sort of concrete jungle of what looked like civic buildings. Many of them seemed half-finished. I pointed this out to Dad and he nodded. 'Typical Iron Curtain architecture, I'm afraid. Grandiose, ugly and inefficient.' Hurriedly he added, 'I expect most of this dates from the bad old Communist days – I imagine things are better now.'

I grinned. No doubt he didn't want to hurt Janos's feelings.

We ended up in a broad, tree-lined boulevard with fountains in the middle and a colossal many-pillared, multi-tiered white building like a cubist wedding cake at the far end.

'Palace of Parliament,' said Janos proudly.

The limousine drove through an arched gateway and pulled into a courtyard. We were shown into a massive entrance hall, and whizzed upwards innumerable stories in an elaborately decorated lift. We emerged into a smaller but equally splendid foyer and were shown into a magnificently furnished office.

At the far end, which looked about half a mile away, a uniformed man sat behind a desk you could have played table tennis on. He jumped to his feet and came forward to greet us.

He was quite a sight. Immensely tall and broad, he had a massive, square-jawed face, with a heavy moustache beneath a beaky nose. He wore an elaborate military uniform, complete with polished jackboots.

'Welcome to Romania,' he bellowed in a voice that rattled the crystal chandelier. 'I am Colonel Roman.'

Sergeant Janos, who had accompanied us into the room, went over to the colonel, came to attention and spoke in a low, urgent voice in what was presumably his native Romanian. He gave me a quick, uneasy glance as he spoke, and I guessed he was describing the incident on the plane, getting his version in first in case we complained.

Colonel Roman growled something back that made Janos turn white and then turned to Dad. In a deep, sinister voice he said, 'I trust that your reception was satisfactory? There were no – problems?'

For once Dad seemed at a loss, so I stepped in. 'None whatsoever,' I said loudly. 'Sergeant Janos received us with the utmost courtesy and correctness.'

Dad said hurriedly, 'This is my son Matthew, colonel. He acts as my assistant – though sometimes I think he thinks it's the other way round.'

'Excellent,' boomed Roman. Waving Janos away he bellowed, 'Drinks!'

A little man hurried in with a laden tray, and

Roman distributed drinks – small glasses of some colourless liquid for him and Dad.

'*Tuica*!' said Roman. 'Plum brandy, very good!'

There was a glass of sweet purple liquid for me. I assumed it was some kind of local cola.

Roman drained his glass in one swallow, and Dad did the same – and then coughed and went red.

Roman slapped him on the back and poured him another, which he sipped more cautiously.

We got down to business, drawing up chairs to Colonel Roman's enormous desk.

'You have seen the file I sent to Ms Alexander, about the death of Doctor Corbie?' he began. 'What do you make of it?'

'Very little, so far,' admitted Dad. 'What was he doing in that little village anyway? I assume his work was here in Bucharest?'

'Holiday,' said Roman briefly. 'He was following your custom – the famous British long weekend.'

'Why that village in particular? Is it especially picturesque?'

'The place is a forsaken hole up in the mountains,' said Roman. 'There is a main street, one shop, a village inn for the peasants, a little river . . .'

'Then why there?' persisted Dad.

Roman hesitated for just a second. 'He was interested in Romanian antiquities.'

'And this village is rich in antiquarian interest?'

'There is nothing in the village but filthy stone hovels.'

'Then why . . . ?'

'He was interested in the castle,' said Roman almost angrily.

'There's a castle in the village?'

'Not *in* the village but above it, in the mountains. Castle Szekuli was once the ancestral home of a great Romanian family. The family died out long ago and the castle is in ruins – but still interesting to an antiquarian – like Corbie.'

'What do you think happened to Doctor Corbie?' asked Dad.

'He was killed by bandits,' said Colonel Roman promptly. 'There are many bandits in that part of the mountains. They try to rob Corbie, he fights back, they cut his throat.'

One thing Dad prides himself on is his power of total recall – and his eye for detail. He'd only flicked through the file, but it was all recorded in his giant brain. 'The report says his throat was ripped, not cut,' he objected.

'Ripped, torn, who cares?' shouted Roman. 'Maybe they used a blunt knife! Maybe they used their teeth, bloody bandits are all barbarians!'

'And the village constable's story? The crouching form – and the bat?'

'Drunk!' said Roman explosively.

'The man was a policeman,' objected Dad.

'He was also an ignorant, drunken peasant, riddled with superstition. He sees a bandit crouching over the body, and thinks it's a vampire bat!'

'The policeman's face was scratched . . .'

'The bandit scratched his face!'

Dad sighed and gave up. He turned to me. 'What do you think, Matthew?'

'I think we might just as well go home,' I said.

Colonel Roman sprang to his feet. 'What are you talking about, boy? Go home? You have only just arrived. Are you not willing to help us?'

'We'd like to, Colonel Roman,' I said. 'But unless you stop lying to us, we're just wasting our time.'

'You dare to say I lie?'

I drew a deep breath and stood my ground. 'Not so much lying as holding things back. You're just not giving us the full story.'

'I am rapidly coming to the same conclusion myself,' said Dad severely. He trotted out one of his favourite Latin tags. *Suppression veri, et suggestio falsi.* Suppressing the truth and suggesting a lie.'

'Why do you insult me?' growled Roman.

'Because you're insulting us,' said Dad calmly.

'I insult you? How?'

'You're insulting our intelligence. You ask us here to investigate Doctor Corbie's death – but you don't really want us to investigate at all. You get angry as soon as we start asking questions about it. You just want us to rubber-stamp your own version of things.'

'Why should I do such a thing?'

'So that you can tell the UN that you sent for an expert and he agreed with all your own conclusions.'

Colonel Roman sat down again, his face twisted with rage and anguish. He was basically honest, I thought, and he knew that what we were saying was true. He just couldn't bear to admit it.

'So why do I do all this?' he said. 'Why do I hide things?'

'Because the things you're not telling us are things you can't bear to talk about,' I said. 'Things you don't want strangers, foreigners like us, to know.'

'And what are these terrible secrets?'

He wanted to tell us, I thought. But he wanted us to say it for him. I looked at Dad, who nodded for me to go on. 'I don't think you would have asked Ms Alexander for our help just because of the death of one foreigner, however important,' I said. 'If people go off to wild, mountainous regions, such things are bound to happen occasionally.'

'Somehow the constable's vampire story got out before you could suppress it,' said Dad. 'The UN got to hear of the murder of a diplomat, and you had to deal with it in some way. So you tried to cope by sending for an expert to investigate it – and discredit the vampire story!'

'The vampire story is rubbish!' growled Roman obstinately. 'Vampires do not exist!'

Dad produced another quotation, slightly adapted this time. ' "Methinks the colonel doth protest too much!" '

'Shakespeare,' I said helpfully. 'Well, almost!'

Roman swung his head from Dad to me, looking very like an angry bull. 'Latin, Shakespeare, what is all this? Talk straight!'

I said, 'He means the reason that you're attacking the constable's vampire story so vigorously is because in your heart of hearts you really believe it's true.'

Colonel Roman gave me an anguished look, but he made no reply.

'So why do you believe it's true?' I asked. 'Not because of this one death – that might very well have been bandits, exactly as you describe. There must have been other deaths, ones you have managed to hush up. Deaths that look like the work of vampires.'

Roman was silent for a moment, staring down at his desk. Then he raised his head. 'Yes, it is true,' he said levelly. 'There have been other deaths. Young girls from the mountain villages, mostly, sometimes young men. Even animals, sometimes. Bodies with their throats torn out, drained of blood. The thing we most fear has happened at last. The vampires have returned to Transylvania!'

For some strange reason an image flashed into my mind. I saw the black-clad, white-faced man who'd been on the plane. I could almost feel his eyes boring into mine . . .

Chapter Four

OUTBREAK

Once he'd decided to come clean, Colonel Roman gave us the whole story.

The killings had started in the mountains of Transylvania just over a year ago. Animals at first and then later human beings. It had taken quite some time for the authorities in distant Bucharest to realise what was going on.

Often the superstitious peasants themselves concealed the deaths. They told hastily-invented stories of accidental falls, sudden fevers or farming accidents. They buried their butchered relatives and friends in their little village grave-yards. No community wanted to be marked with the taint of vampirism.

When the authorities did discover what was going on they were horrified at the extent of the killings – and they were almost as panic-stricken as the peasants themselves.

'It is bad enough that the foreign tourists must come on their stupid Dracula tours,' said Colonel Roman. Like many Romanians, he was excessively sensitive about his country's association with Count Dracula and the vampire legend.

'They enjoy shuddering as they visit what they believe to be the castle of Count Dracula, someone who never really existed,' he went on angrily. 'But real vampires, real deaths – in a country with ambitions to join the European Union? It is a disaster!'

Police and security forces had been ordered to conceal the very existence of the problem while the authorities tried to work out a method of dealing with it.

'I can understand how you feel,' said Dad. 'You'd have journalists and TV camera units from all over the world turning up if the story ever got out.'

'And we would be branded worldwide as primitive and bloodthirsty barbarians,' said Roman savagely. 'The legend of the vampire has held our country back for hundreds of years.'

'It's pretty surprising that you managed to keep things so quiet for so long,' I said.

Colonel Roman smiled grimly. 'This country was a dictatorship for many years, and old habits die hard. Few people care to disobey the security police. It is not very democratic, but it can be very useful!'

The death of Doctor Corbie had threatened to blow the lid off things. As Dad had realised, we'd been brought in to help discredit any rumours about vampires.

Now that he knew the score, Dad wasn't standing for any more nonsense. 'If we're to stay you must let us make a thorough and genuine investigation. Otherwise, as Matthew said, we might as well go straight back home.'

Colonel Roman looked dubious. I suppose a lifelong habit of secrecy is hard to break.

'It will be a very discreet investigation,' I promised. 'Whatever we discover we'll report only to you and, in due course, to Ms Alexander – and she won't talk.'

Roman considered for a moment longer. Then he looked up. 'Word of an Englishman?' he said solemnly.

'Word of an Englishman,' said Dad, equally seriously.

They stood up and shook hands. I stood up and shook hands as well. Then we all sat down again and started to make plans.

'Where do you begin?' asked Roman.

'Where the unfortunate Doctor Corbie ended, I suppose,' said Dad.

'In the village of Szekuli.'

'You mentioned a castle,' I said.

Roman nodded. 'Castle Szekuli.'

'Was there any particular reason Doctor Corbie was so interested in it?'

Roman sighed. 'Like so many Westerners, Corbie had a morbid interest in our vampire legends.'

'Go on.'

'Castle Szekuli is the ancient home of the Szekuli family.'

'And?'

'The Szekuli were believed by local people to be vampires,' said Roman reluctantly. 'One day the peasants stormed Castle Szekuli, burned it down and killed all of the Szekuli family they could find.'

'I take it all this happened in the Middle Ages,' said Dad.

Roman shook his head. 'It happened ninety years ago. Everyone thought the Szekuli were the last vampires in Transylvania.'

'Were all the Szekuli killed?' I asked.

'Who knows?' Roman laughed grimly. 'Since our counter-revolution many aristos have come back to claim their property. Maybe Count Szekuli has come back as well!'

I shuddered. 'Maybe he has.'

'I shall send you to Szekuli in my official car,' said Roman. 'Sergeant Janos will go with you as interpreter – and bodyguard.'

'Er – perhaps not,' I said.

Colonel Roman raised an eyebrow. 'You don't like Janos?'

'It's not that – but nobody could take Janos for anything but a secret policeman. We might do better if people aren't too frightened to talk to us.'

Dad frowned. 'We shall still need an interpreter.'

'I know.' I turned to Colonel Roman. 'Any chance you could find us someone who doesn't look as if they were in the secret police? And a less impressive car? Something a tourist might hire here in Bucharest?'

Roman thought for a moment. 'The car is no problem. As for the interpreter . . .' Suddenly he beamed. 'I have the perfect interpreter. Tonight you will dine with me, hotel restaurant at seven. I shall bring the interpreter . . .'

The Hotel Magnifici in Academii Street more than lived up to its name. It was a huge and magnificent building recently restored to five-star status. As honoured guests of the state, Dad and I shared a stunningly luxurious two-bedroomed suite.

'Make the most of it,' said Dad drily. 'We'll probably be sleeping in the village inn at Szekuli tomorrow.'

'Straw mattresses and bedbugs,' I said. 'Vampire bedbugs, I shouldn't wonder!'

We bathed and changed – the bath was big enough to swim in – and at seven we went down to the restaurant to meet Colonel Roman.

We reached the foyer just in time to see him arrive in an official limousine. He was wearing an even more splendid uniform this time – and he was accompanied by one of the most stunning young women I've ever seen. She wore some kind of little black dress and she was tall and slim, with jet-black hair, very white skin and sparkling black eyes.

'My daughter Magda,' said Colonel Roman. 'Your interpreter.'

He caught my stunned look and grinned. 'Is the suggested interpreter acceptable? Not too like a secret policeman?'

'The suggested interpreter is . . . terrific,' I stammered. 'Not a bit like a secret policeman.'

We went into dinner. We ate a large and splendid meal in the hotel's large and splendid restaurant. Colonel Roman chose the meal – a selection of local specialities, all delicious and all unpronounceable.

There were glittering crystal chandeliers and glittering, rich-looking people everywhere you looked, and about seventeen waiters were per-petually dancing around our table. Whatever the country's economic problems, some Romanians were doing very well.

I noticed lots of people eyeing our table, and wondered if they were doing so because Magda was so beautiful, or because Colonel Roman was so important.

Dad and Colonel Roman did most of the

talking, although I eventually regained the use of my tongue enough to attempt some conversation with Magda. Her English was excellent, although over-formal, rather like her manner. She seemed a serious-minded girl, quite like her father, and although she was a pleasure to look at, I didn't think she was going to be many laughs.

Still, she was a lot prettier than Sergeant Janos.

It turned out that she was a secret police person after all, working as her father's assistant – which was only to be expected. I'd already gathered from Wainwright's briefing that nepotism was a way of life in Romania.

We were at the coffee stage when I suddenly got that feeling in the back of my neck again. I turned and there he was, sitting alone at a corner table. Tall, white-faced, staring at me – at all of us – with those burning eyes. I turned away, trying to ignore him.

Dad noticed my abstraction. 'Something wrong, Matthew?'

It didn't seem the moment to go into it, so I said, 'Sorry, must be jet-lag or something . . .'

Soon after that the party broke up and Dad and I went back to our suite. I said goodnight to

Dad, went to my own bedroom and got into bed.

I couldn't get to sleep. I suddenly realised I was far from home and in an unfamiliar country. I had the sense of a dark landscape of mountains and forests pressing in on me outside the luxury of the bedroom.

I still felt as if someone was watching me. And I suddenly felt frightened.

Feeling a complete and utter idiot, I put on the bedside light, got out of bed and padded across the deep pile carpet to the luggage rack by the door. I fished deep inside my suitcase and pulled out a couple of cloves of garlic and the reproduction of the cross of Saint Thingummyjig.

Checking that my bedroom door was locked and my window closed, I put the garlic cloves on the floor in front of the door and retired to bed clutching my reproduction crucifix. I just hoped I woke up in time to move the garlic before Dad came in. If he caught sight of either garlic or crucifix I'd never hear the last of it.

Even with all my precautions I still couldn't get off to sleep, not properly anyway. I drifted in and out of an uneasy doze, never quite sure if I was awake or asleep.

Suddenly I heard soft footsteps padding outside my door. I watched in horror as the door – the locked door – opened silently. A tall, black shape appeared in the doorway, stepped into my room – and then jumped back with a hiss of rage.

Good old garlic, I thought. He didn't reckon on that!

Suddenly I was wide awake, and shaking with fear. I jumped out of bed and tried the door. It was still firmly locked.

Telling myself I must have dreamed the whole thing, I got back into bed. I told myself I was a fool for giving myself nightmares. All this vampire stuff must be getting to me. No more Hammer Horrors, I thought sleepily. Once again I started drifting into sleep . . .

This time I was woken by the chimes of some nearby clock. I began to count the chimes, somehow knowing what the total would be . . .

Ten . . . eleven . . . twelve . . .

Midnight.

Long velvet curtains covered the window beside my bed. Suddenly they began billowing in the breeze. But the window was closed . . .

Suddenly the curtains were flung back and

I saw a tall, black shape standing in the window. I caught a glimpse of red eyes in a white face as the shape sprang towards me. Claw-like hands reached out for me, red eyes glowed and I saw white pointed teeth. I gave a yell of fear.

Fumbling under my pillow I grabbed the crucifix and thrust it at the figure like a sword. With an angry hiss the figure shot backwards towards the window and vanished.

I jumped out of bed and stood shaking beside it as Dad rushed through the adjoining door and into the room. He switched on the light. 'What is it, Matthew, another nightmare?'

'I'm not sure . . . I thought someone was in my room.'

I went over to the window. It was still closed. I opened it and looked out. There was a low, broad balcony, with other balconies above, below and beside it.

Dad came and looked out of the window. 'We were warned that there was a lot of crime in Bucharest. I suppose an exceptionally agile hotel thief could have managed to climb in.'

'Yes, that's what it must have been,' I said. 'A hotel thief.'

'Odd that he should close the window behind him, though,' said Dad. 'Shall I get the management to call the police?'

I shook my head. 'Too much red tape, and they'd never catch him. Let's just forget it; we're leaving tomorrow anyway.'

I eventually persuaded Dad to go back to bed.

Once he was gone I closed the window and put one of the cloves of garlic under it, leaving the other cloves by the door. I sat up in bed, clutching my crucifix and waiting for dawn.

Next morning, after a hearty breakfast, we went down and waited for Magda and Colonel Roman in the hotel foyer.

As the hotel staff put our luggage in Magda's modest saloon car I turned to Colonel Roman. 'Could you do me a favour?'

'Anything, my young friend.'

'I'd like a look at the hotel register.'

We went over to reception and a few short, sharp words from Colonel Roman produced the register without argument. I looked at last night's page, and there, next to ours, was the name I'd been expecting: *Count Nikolai Szekuli*.

It looked as if the heir to Castle Szekuli had returned to claim his property. I wondered if he'd be waiting there to meet us when we arrived . . .

Chapter Five

THE PATIENT

Thanks to my eventful night I saw very little of the journey into Transylvania. I was asleep in the back of the car most of the way. Dad and Magda sat in the front taking turns with the driving.

Occasionally I awoke for a minute or two and got a hazy impression of rolling green fields divided by little hedges, of lakes and forests with mountains in the background. By the time I woke up properly it was early evening and we were driving through the concrete suburbs of a little town called Bracav.

Apparently it was the nearest town of any size to the mountain village of Szekuli, and Magda had decided against driving unfamiliar mountain roads after dark.

'We can stay here tonight and go on to Szekuli in the morning,' she said. 'There will be an inn of sorts here, not like the Hotel Magnifici, but adequate. If you do not object to simple accommodation for once . . .'

We hastened to assure her that we didn't insist on five-star luxury every night. 'Anywhere with a bed and a roof,' said Dad.

'And food,' I said. Apparently they'd stopped for a picnic lunch but I'd slept right through it and I was starving.

Magda drove through the horrible new suburbs and into the picturesque old town, where she found us a nice old-fashioned hotel. Stone-flagged floors, whitewashed walls and ceilings, old wooden beams, and a white-haired, red-faced landlord, who kept bowing and smiling. Tourists seemed to be valued in Bracav.

The place looked strangely familiar – and suddenly it came to me. It was exactly like the picturesque village inn in all those old Hammer Horror vampire movies. You know, the one where the terrified landlord warns the young traveller not to go on to Castle Dracula – or possibly Castle Frankenstein – after dark. The place where the stable-boy rushes into the bar to say yet another local virgin in a low-necked peasant blouse has gone missing.

We had an early dinner in the little dining-room. More *specialitile regiuni* including *pirjoale*, which turned out to be rissoles, and *pui Cimpulungean*, chicken stuffed with bacon and sausage. It had a strong flavour of garlic as well, which reassured me about staying at the inn. If I did get attacked by a vampire I'd just breathe on him.

Feeling a little foolish I surreptitiously slipped my hands into my jacket pockets. Cloves of garlic in one pocket, crucifix in the other. Foolish or not, from now on I wasn't going to go anywhere without them.

At the end of the meal Dad had sudden inspiration. 'Isn't Bracav the place where that policeman was hospitalised?' he said, displaying his amazing power of total recall. 'The one who found Doctor Corbie's body.'

Magda fished inside the enormous shoulder bag which never left her, produced the file and consulted it. 'That is so.'

'Is he still here?'

She looked at the file again. 'I believe so. The file has been kept up to date and there is no mention of his being discharged.'

'It might be useful to talk to him,' said Dad thoughtfully.

Magda frowned. 'He gives a full report of the events in his statement. It is all here, in the file.'

'It could still be useful to get a first-hand account,' I said. 'He may have recalled something else by now, something which didn't get into the file.'

Magda's expression made it clear that she thought this very unlikely, but she was prepared to humour our strange Western ideas – however ridiculous. 'We can certainly see the man if you wish.'

'Perhaps you could ring the hospital for us?' suggested Dad. 'Maybe we can make an appointment for the morning.'

Looking beautiful but determined, Magda shook her head. 'We still have some way to go into the mountains. Tomorrow I wish to make an early start.'

Magda had a tendency to be bossy, but she'd met her match in Dad.

'That's as may be, young lady. But I must insist on talking to that policeman before we leave Bracav.'

Magda stood up. 'Then we shall go now!'

Dad was obviously feeling sluggish after the local *specialitile* – not to mention the local red wine. He looked at his watch. 'It's getting rather late. Will the hospital let us see the man at this hour?'

Magda looked at him in mild surprise. 'We can see whoever we wish, whenever we wish. We have passes from the Securitate.'

Magda seemed to think that being in the Securitate was the same as being medieval royalty. You just announced what you wanted and everyone fell over themselves to get it for you.

She checked the hospital address in the file and its location on her street-map and we set off in the car. The hospital wasn't hard to find. It was a square white building on a hill at the edge of town.

Seeing it reminded me of the old joke from the *Airplane* movie. I turned to Magda. 'There's a message from the hospital.'

She looked at me in astonishment. 'How can there be?'

'No, no,' I said. 'You have to say, "What is it?" '
I tried again. 'There's a message from the hospital.'

Obediently Magda said, 'What is it?'

'It's a big, white building with doctors and nurses!'

She didn't laugh. 'This is an English joke?'

'American, actually,' I said. 'But never mind that now.'

We pulled up outside the hospital and went inside, finding ourselves in a bare lobby gleaming with polish. There was a large, dragon-like female behind the reception desk. She looked at us in outrage and rattled off something sharp in Romanian, obviously telling us to get lost.

But Magda had been quite right about the power of the Securitate. A few even sharper words in reply, plus a flash of the Securitate pass, reduced the dragon to a quivering jelly. She grabbed the reception telephone and produced a junior doctor, still shrugging himself into his white coat.

Magda explained our mission and soon we were being shown along a shining white corridor to a locked room with a grille in the door. The doctor slid back the grille and we looked through. An incredibly emaciated, unshaven man in a hospital gown was lying on the little iron bed, staring at the night sky through a small, barred window.

Through Magda, Dad asked the doctor about the man's condition. Apparently he had been wild and violent when first brought in and had then lapsed into a coma. For a while they had feared he had blood poisoning from the scratch on his forehead, but that seemed to have subsided and for several weeks he had been passive and apathetic. He was considered harmless now, locked up only for his own safety.

Dad asked about his appetite and was told that the man ate ferociously, always cleaning his plate and demanding more. Curiously enough, he never seemed to put on weight. In fact, he'd grown thinner since entering the hospital.

The young doctor opened the door, and we went into the room. The doctor wanted to stay but Magda chased him away, presumably for security reasons, and we started the questioning. At first the man refused to answer. Magda spoke sharply to him and produced her Securitate pass.

The man was a policeman after all, and I suppose he recognised the voice of authority. Anyway, he started to answer.

Speaking through Magda, Dad took him

through the events of the evening. He told the story exactly as he had in the statement on the file. The midnight patrol, the strange growling sound, the dark shape crouching over the body outside the shop . . .

'Ask if he's sure he hit the shape when he fired at it,' I said.

Magda put the question, and the policeman answered emphatically, nodding his head.

'He says he is sure. He shot it twice, but bullets had no effect,' said Magda.

'*Strigoi*,' muttered the man. '*Strigoi!*'

Magda said something soothing, and turned back to us. 'He says it was a vampire.'

'And I'm sure he believes it, poor fellow,' said Dad. 'Unfortunately we've learned nothing new. I'm afraid you were right, Magda – this visit has been a waste of time.'

'I will call the doctor,' said Magda. She began moving towards the door.

I was watching the man on the bed. He seemed almost unaware of us now. He was sitting hunched up, knees under his chin, staring out of the little barred window high in the wall. I followed his gaze and saw the full moon come out from behind a black cloud. The man tensed, and then there was a sort of coiled-spring quality about his stillness. A red glare came into his eyes.

Suddenly he seemed to fly from the bed, hurtling through the air towards Magda.

Subconsciously I must have been expecting something like this to happen. Without thinking, I shoulder-charged him in midair, knocking him off-course. Unfortunately I knocked him straight into Dad.

The force of the impact sent Dad sprawling back on the bed with the man on top of him. Lips drawn back, his attacker snapped at Dad's throat. Dad reached out and grabbed his skinny shoulders, desperate to hold him off.

Now Dad's quite a big chap and he should have been able to hold off his emaciated attacker with ease. But he couldn't. The man grabbed Dad's shoulders and began pulling himself closer – closer to Dad's throat.

I ran to help and Magda joined in. We had no effect at all. The man's skinny arms felt like steel cables and his pointed teeth came ever nearer the pulse that was beating in Dad's throat . . .

Chapter Six

THE VILLAGE OF SZEKULI

Almost too late, I realised what I had to do.

Letting go, I fished one of my cloves of garlic from my pocket and smashed it into the thin man's forehead. As the juice from the crushed clove touched his skin the man gave a terrible scream, let go of Dad and sprang back from the bed, clawing desperately at his own forehead.

Then he swung round, claw-like hands reaching out, and advanced towards me . . .

I backed away, reaching in my pocket . . .

He was about to spring when I took the crucifix from my pocket and thrust it in his face. He froze, and then backed away, snarling.

'Get help!' I yelled. 'Quickly! I'm not sure how long this will work.'

By now Magda was already shouting down the corridor.

Dad scrambled up from the bed and came to stand at my side, ready to meet the next attack.

I could feel the man striving against the power of the crucifix. I thrust it nearer and he backed away – then started to move forward again . . .

Footsteps came pounding down the corridor and two hospital orderlies burst into the room, the young doctor behind them. The orderlies were both big men but it took all their combined strength to hold the frantically writhing policeman down long enough for the doctor to give him a massive injection. It took a long time to work, but at last he fell back on to the bed, unconscious.

I touched Dad on the arm. 'Look at his forehead.'

We leaned over the sleeping form. Where the garlic juice had touched the policeman's skin there was a livid red weal.

Dad got Magda to ask for a pair of rubber gloves. When they arrived he put them on and pulled back the unconscious man's lips. Two of the front teeth were longer and more pointed than the others.

'Abnormal development of the canines,' said

Dad. 'I thought as much. I got a very close look at those teeth just now.'

He lifted one of the man's skinny arms, pushing back the sleeve.

'Abnormal muscular development . . .'

'Abnormal reflexes too,' I said. 'Did you see how fast he came off of that bed when he went for Magda?'

Dad nodded and borrowed a stethoscope from the young doctor and listened to the man's chest (he'd picked up a medical degree sometime to go with all his others, although he's never practised). He listened for a moment, took the stethoscope off and handed it to me.

I had no idea what a healthy heart was supposed to sound like – but I was pretty sure that this steadily frantic pounding wasn't normal.

'Hyperactive metabolism,' said Dad. 'That would account for the constant hunger, the weight-loss and the abnormal physical strength.'

He handed the stethoscope back to the doctor, peeled off the rubber gloves and stepped back from the bed, his eyes shining with the pure excitement of scientific discovery. 'Do you know what we're dealing with here, Matthew?

Vampirism isn't a primitive superstition. It's a disease, transmitted by contagion of the blood!'

He looked a bit disappointed when I just nodded. 'You don't seem very surprised,' he said reproachfully. 'This is a tremendously important breakthrough!'

'I think I was beginning to suspect something of the sort,' I said. 'I hadn't quite put it together. They used to burn the bodies to ash, you know. And some of the old accounts speak of "epidemics" of vampirism.'

Dad turned to Magda. 'Tell these people that this man must be kept under guard, and in strict isolation. Then call your father and tell him that the patient must be taken to the finest hospital in Bucharest, and examined by experts in diseases of the blood. They may be able to find a cure, perhaps even a preventive vaccine. I know some people in England and in America who might help.'

Magda shot a stream of instructions at the doctor and the orderlies. We went back to the hospital foyer, where she commandeered a telephone and had a long conversation with her father back in Bucharest.

At last she put down the phone. 'My father will see to it, Professor Stirling. He asks what we will do now.'

'We still have to discover why the disease has suddenly sprung up again.'

I nodded. 'I've got a feeling we'll find the answer to that at Castle Szekuli.'

We went back to the inn and sat up talking over Dad's great scientific discovery.

'The disease must have appeared in the Middle Ages, like the plague,' said Dad. 'Just like the plague it eventually burned itself out – except for pockets lying dormant here and there.'

'Don't lots of diseases do that?' I asked. 'Make a comeback just when you think you've got them licked?'

Dad nodded. 'I'm afraid they do. It's happening now with malaria, and with tuberculosis. And of course, the causes of diseases can be incredibly long-lived. Anthrax spores can be still infectious after being buried for hundreds of years.'

'Maybe the spores of vampirism were buried in the ruins of Castle Szekuli,' I said. 'People got infected somehow and the disease spread.'

Magda frowned, still not entirely convinced. 'If vampirism is a disease, as you say, professor, why does it give the victims this terrible hunger for human blood?'

'They need the nourishment,' said Dad simply. 'The boosted metabolism produces a constant craving for food – especially protein. And it isn't just human blood, remember. According to your father, animals were attacked as well.'

'But why does garlic have such an effect? Why do vampires hate sunlight and running water?'

'The disease must produce an allergic reaction to garlic,' said Dad. 'Sunlight – well, maybe the skin becomes extra sensitive to ultraviolet rays. As for the running water – perhaps the illness has some of the characteristics of hydrophobia.'

'What about their fear of crucifixes?' I asked.

Dad shrugged. 'There, I admit, I'm baffled.'

Magda said solemnly, 'Perhaps you are right, Professor Stirling, and vampirism is a disease. But here in Transylvania it is not just a disease. It is a part of the local culture, mixed up with tradition, superstition – and with religion. The sufferer from vampirism believes that he is evil, cursed –

damned. No wonder the cross, the symbol of the church, of goodness, causes such fear.'

'And the connection with bats?' I asked. 'That policeman said he was actually infected by a bat, remember.'

'Perhaps bats get the disease as well,' suggested Dad. 'We know that different forms of some diseases are common to humans and animals.'

'Like BSE, for instance . . .' I suggested.

'Exactly. Bats may infect humans – or even the other way round.'

'Vampire bats do exist though, don't they?'

'Most certainly. But as far as we know, you only find them in the tropics. And they're pretty mild creatures – they feed mostly on cattle.'

'Do they ever attack humans?'

Dad shrugged. 'They might suck a few drops of blood from your toe if it sticks out from under your mosquito net while you're asleep.'

'They may have a different kind of vampire bat over here,' I said. I remembered another piece of vampire lore – the most famous of all. 'What about the traditional stake through the heart?'

Dad considered for a moment. 'I only made a superficial examination of that poor man, but you saw how quick he was, how extraordinarily strong. Someone like that would be very hard to kill. He might survive wounds that would destroy an ordinary human. I think all the stake through the heart means is that to kill a vampire you have to deliver a massive wound in a vital spot.'

'Beheading was another recommended method,' I said.

'Yes, that would do it,' said Dad thoughtfully.

Our heads full of night horrors, we went reluctantly to bed.

Next morning we set off for the mountain village of Szekuli. It was a longish drive and a difficult one towards the end, over narrow mountain roads, rutted and potholed and winding ever upwards.

I was glad Magda had insisted on an early start. It didn't sound like the sort of place you wanted to arrive in after dark.

All through the long drive I was thinking about our discovery that vampirism was a disease. I could see desperate, infected victims wandering the countryside, filled with a devouring hunger that made them kill people and drink their blood. I could see them falling into comas, being taken for dead, and buried – and then reviving, and crawling from their graves to feed again.

The theory explained much – but not every-thing.

In particular, it didn't explain the man who had followed us, and my strange experiences at the Hotel Magnifici. It didn't explain Count Szekuli. I had an uneasy feeling that I wouldn't know the full truth until we met again. It was something I looked forward to and dreaded at the same time.

Soon we were approaching a little village in a narrow mountain pass. Looming above it was a ruined castle.

Castle Szekuli, the count's ancestral home.

Like the inn back in Bracav, the castle looked strangely familiar. The reason, I soon realised, was the same. It was the same Dracula's castle I had seen in countless old horror movies: a jumble of crooked battlements, turrets and towers perched high on a mountain crag.

Some of the towers had collapsed, and a sizeable chunk of the castle had crumbled away and fallen down the mountainside. Being partly ruined didn't make the castle any less impressive. It just added to its air of sinister horror.

We drove up the steep main street of the village without seeing a soul. The houses were much as Colonel Roman had described them – grimy stone hovels. There was a solitary shop – some kind of general store – down one of the sidestreets, but its door was shut and its windows shuttered.

We drove up to the little square at the top of the street and parked outside the village inn. It was a smaller version of the one back in Bracav, not clean and bright but gloomy and depressing. No whitewash, just grimy blackened stone.

Instead of a smiling host there was a wizened old crone who looked as if she'd parked her broomstick round the back. I think she tried to turn us away, but a few sharp words from Magda plus a massive bundle of lei from the black shoulder bag did the trick. It looked as if Magda was handing over a fortune, but since there are well over a thousand lei to the pound it was probably about a tenner.

We were shown to three scruffy little rooms, each containing an iron bedstead complete with dirty blankets and a washstand with jug and basin. Toilet facilities, such as they were, were out at the back.

The rooms provoked another rattle of angry Romanian from Magda and some more lei appeared from the black bag.

'The place is a pigsty,' said Magda, 'but it is all there is. The old woman has promised to clean the rooms. Also, she will provide us with some kind of hot meal.'

Yes, but what kind? I wondered. Still, it was late afternoon by now and we'd pushed on to reach Szekuli without stopping, so the idea of hot food was welcome. I decided not to think about the kitchen.

Once we'd chucked our cases in the rooms, we went along to look at the scene of the crime, outside the shuttered sidestreet shop. There appeared to be no trace left of the incident, not even a bloodstain on the road.

A thought struck me and I examined the heavy wooden shutters outside the shop. There was a round mark near the top, a kind of scar. It was just low enough for me to reach. I produced my Swiss Army knife, and dug at the mark with the knife-blade. I reached up and pulled out a piece of twisted grey metal.

'The policeman's bullet,' I said. 'I bet he missed by a mile both times! No telling where the other shot went.'

Since there seemed nothing more to be learned we went back to the inn.

Dinner was served in the gloomy dining-room with wooden benches at a battered wooden table. The food was surprisingly good, a sort of all-purpose stew served in bowls from a big iron pot. Magda said it was called Transylvanian hotpot.

There was coarse, greyish bread, and a jug of rough red wine. Dad said you could have used it to unblock drains. He managed to empty the jug all the same.

When the meal was over Dad said, 'I don't think there's anything more to be learned in the village.'

Magda said, 'The old woman says most villagers moved away after the foreigner's death. There isn't even a new policeman yet.'

'Just one last job to do then,' said Dad. 'While we're here I think we ought to take a quick look at that castle.'

'What about the danger of infection?' I asked.

'The disease is only transmitted through contaminated blood. As long as we're careful we should be all right.'

Dad's always ready to risk everything for science, but I wasn't nearly so keen. 'If we're going to the castle we should be sure to get back before dark,' I said. 'We don't want to be stumbling around those ruins at midnight.'

Magda stood up. 'Then let us go at once.'

'Not you, Magda,' said Dad. 'You're staying here.'

Magda was outraged. 'Professor Stirling, I must insist . . .'

'No, I insist,' snapped Dad. 'I'm responsible for you to your father – and yesterday we could have got you killed. Besides, just suppose something does happen to us – not that it will, but just suppose – we'll need you here to report to your father and see that the investigation is carried on.'

It took a lot more arguing, but at last Magda agreed to stay behind. It was the appeal to duty that finally convinced her.

As we set off for the castle, I said, 'You just want to keep Magda out of danger, don't you?'

He looked at me in surprise. 'Well of course I

do, Matthew. Things may get a bit sticky, it's no place for a girl.'

I told you he was old-fashioned.

We began climbing the steep mountain track that led up to Castle Szekuli.

Chapter Seven

THE LAST VAMPIRE

It was no easy task climbing up to Castle Szekuli.

The path was so steep that sometimes it seemed almost vertical. It was strewn with rocks and boulders you had to climb over or round. They slowed down our rate of progress no end, and it took far more time than we'd allowed for to reach the head of the pass and the narrow crumbling bridge that led to the castle.

I looked at my watch. 'We'd better get a move on,' I said. 'There can't be too much daylight left.'

'Time for a quick look around,' said Dad confidently – too confidently for my liking.

I hesitated. 'I don't like the look of that bridge much.'

The castle had been built on a detached pinnacle of rock, shaped rather like a giant lighthouse. The deep chasm that divided the mountain and the castle itself was spanned by a stone bridge. Stone walls set with spear-like iron spikes bordered the sides of the bridge – or at least, they used to. The wall to the left had crumbled away – you could see the remains of it far below, a jumble of stone blocks and iron spikes.

'Nothing to worry about,' said Dad. 'It's only one side of the bridge wall that's gone. The structure of the bridge itself isn't damaged. If we keep to the good side we'll be fine.' Keeping well over to the right, he marched across the bridge, and I had no alternative but to follow.

The bridge certainly felt solid enough as we marched across. On the other side was a paved courtyard and beyond that the main doors of the castle, now crumbled and fallen away.

We crossed the courtyard and went inside. We found ourselves in a ruined hall, empty except for the remains of a great wooden table, its timbers blackened with smoke, and a few fragments of charred and rotting tapestries on the wall. The hall was gloomy, illuminated only by the light from the doorway, and from a few narrow windows in its walls.

A stone staircase wound round a central pillar, emerging from the stone floor and disappearing through the ceiling above.

There was litter under the table and I went to examine it.

'Some of this stuff looks recent. There are wine bottles, bones with meat on, even a few empty tins. It looks as if people have been living here.'

'Tramps, or bandits,' said Dad.

'Or vampires,' I said. 'Who else would live here?'

Dad looked at the staircase. 'Up or down?'

'Well, I don't fancy the basement much,' I said.

We climbed the spiral staircase and explored the upper levels. There was little to see, just a series of empty stone chambers, without even the litter I'd found below.

We climbed another level and found open sky overhead. Most of the tower's roof had crumbled away, and several of the rooms had lost their outer walls. It all looked far too dangerous, and the light was fading fast. It was already dusk.

'Time to go, I think,' said Dad and we went back down the stairway to the main hall.

It wasn't empty any more.

A group of ragged, grimy figures stood round

the bottom of the staircase. They were skeleton-thin like the policeman in the hospital, with burning eyes and claw-like hands.

They were vampires.

Not tall and elegant like Count Dracula, but thin and grimy, desperate and starving like wild animals. They were almost pathetic, but their devouring hunger made them deadly dangerous. They were hungry for our blood.

I looked at Dad. 'Told you so,' I said, trying to keep my voice steady. 'They must live in the cellars underneath the castle. They come out when it starts getting dark.'

And when they get hungry, I thought.

'Well, it's always nice to be proved right,' said Dad grimly. 'What do you suggest we do now?'

'Leave!' I said and took the crucifix from my pocket. I waved it round me in a circle and the vampires fell back.

We moved towards the door and the vampires moved with us, keeping their distance but following us in a rough semicircle. We went through the door and out into the courtyard.

'Maybe they won't leave the castle,' I said. 'If we can get over the bridge . . .'

But the bridge was barred.

The figure barring it wasn't thin and ragged like the other vampires. He was tall and elegant, black-cloaked, white-faced, with burning red eyes.

He was Count Nikolai Szekuli.

'Welcome to my ancestral home,' he said. His voice was deep and mellow, and his English held only the slightest trace of accent.

'I am afraid you are not seeing it at its best,' he went on. 'Which is unfortunate, since it is the last place you will ever see. I taught that fool Corbie not to meddle in my affairs when he came prying here. Now it seems I must teach you!'

'Don't be too sure of that, Count Nikolai,' I said, and raised the crucifix.

He gave a blood-curdling laugh. 'How long do you think you can hold us all back with that ridiculous symbol? Soon the sun will go down, the moon will rise and my people will grow strong. And there are my other servants.'

He gave a high-pitched, almost inaudible whistle and a cloud of bats rose from the ruined towers, swirled around for a moment and then returned. I wondered if he'd trained them to attack . . .

Dad, who'd been unusually silent, said indignantly, 'Do I take it you know this man, Matthew?'

'He followed us from London,' I said. 'And I think he tried to kill me at the Magnifici Hotel in Bucharest.' I raised my voice, addressing the count. 'Why? What have you got against us? And come to that, how did you know about us anyway?'

'I have important friends, fellow exiles, in London. I learned that you were being sent to track me down. So I came back to London and tracked *you*!'

'I know who you are, Count Nikolai,' I said. 'But what are you? Where do you fit into all this?'

'I am the hereditary ruler of these people, an aristocrat of the pure vampire race. Years ago we were hunted down and driven from our rightful place. For long years I lived in exile in London. Then I heard that the vampires had returned to Transylvania. Now I too have returned to lead my people.'

Dad was studying him with scientific interest. 'You appear very different from these other – specimens.'

'They are peasants,' said Count Nikolai scornfully. 'I am an aristocrat. I am what the vampire can become, once it has evolved into a superior being. I have powers these scum never dreamed of. *I* do not fear the daylight as these do. I can pass any barrier, dominate the minds of men . . .'

'You scorn your – associates. Yet you wish to lead them?'

'They are a nucleus, the beginnings of a vampire army. They will create others, those others will create still others, until we rule Transylvania once more. Then all Romania, then Europe and then the world!'

'You know, I pity you,' said Dad. He waved at the ragged vampires who were shuffling closer, centimetre by centimetre. 'These poor people are sick, but you're not sick, you're mad. And in your madness you exploit their weakness.'

'Enough!' shrieked Nikolai. 'Soon the sun will have set – and you will be in my power.'

Even as he spoke, the sky seemed to darken. The semicircle of vampires closed in, forcing us towards the bridge – and towards Count Nikolai.

'Prepare to die!' screamed Nikolai.

Suddenly, to my horror, I saw a familiar

figure appear round the mountain path. It was Magda, as neat and as beautiful as ever, the giant bag over her shoulder.

'Magda, run!' I yelled. 'Get away from here, it's a nest of vampires!'

Count Nikolai whirled round to face her, but Magda didn't run. She came to a halt on the other side of the bridge. She reached into the shoulder bag and produced the biggest automatic I have ever seen. Raising it in a very professional-looking two-handed grip, she aimed it at Count Nikolai.

'Stupid girl!' he screamed. 'Don't you know who I am – what I am? Do you think any ordinary weapon can harm me?'

'Yes, I do,' said Magda calmly. 'Provided, of course, that Professor Stirling's theories about vampirism are correct . . . This is no ordinary weapon. It is an Israeli Desert Eagle Automatic, 8mm, ten-shot, manufactured by Uzi. It is the most powerful handgun ever made.'

For one glorious moment I thought she was going to say, 'Make my day, punk!' or even, 'Do you feel lucky?' Instead she went on, 'It is loaded with explosive bullets!'

She swung the gun round and fired at the

bridge's remaining side wall. There was a deafening report and a colossal chunk of masonry was blasted away.

Already the gun was once more aiming at Count Nikolai. 'Surrender, and order those others to surrender,' said Magda. 'Believe me, if I shoot you with this gun, you will die.'

'It is you who will die!' screamed Nikolai.

To my horror he began dashing across the bridge towards her, moving with the incredible speed of the vampire, weaving to and fro to confuse her aim.

'Magda, shoot him!' I yelled.

She fired, not at Nikolai, but at his feet.

I don't think she was trying to kill him. It was a warning shot – but the end result was the same. The bullet hit the bridge at Nikolai's feet, when he was running along the side without a wall. A huge chunk of bridge vanished from beneath his feet and Nikolai twisted sideways, toppling over the unprotected side of the bridge.

Arms and legs flailing wildly, he toppled down into the chasm below, landing, with a kind of inevitability, on one of the metal spikes that stuck up through the rubble. The force of the impact drove the metal stake through his heart.

Dad and I dashed across the bridge and the troupe of ragged vampires rushed angrily after us.

As they advanced across the bridge, Magda fired a burst of explosive bullets over their heads and at their feet. They turned and fled screaming back into the castle.

We moved cautiously to the edge of the bridge and looked down at Count Nikolai's transfixed body far below us.

'He was an evil man,' said Magda sadly, 'but I did not wish to kill him.'

I patted her awkwardly on the back. 'Never mind,' I said. 'It's the way he'd have wanted to go!'

Shaken but relieved we moved away, glad to leave the castle behind us. As we set off down the mountain path, I said, 'You know, Magda, you got it all wrong.'

'I did?'

'You're the heroine. You're supposed to scream when you see the monster and wait for us to come and rescue you, not the other way round!'

'Times change,' said Magda solemnly.

I looked at Dad. 'What was it you said? "Things may get a bit sticky, it's no place for a girl." '

He looked a bit shamefaced, which is unusual for him. 'Well, Matthew, as Magda said, times change . . .'

We made good time on the way back to the inn. Despite the darkness, it was easier going down and there was the thought of the remaining vampires behind us to spur us on.

When we reached the village inn, Magda produced a military-looking field-radio from the shoulder bag. She had a long, impassioned conversation in Romanian, reporting to her father back in Bucharest.

Then we chucked our luggage into the car, climbed in after it and drove away.

As Magda drove us down the steep mountain road, Dad said, 'Something will have to be done about that tower and its remaining occupants.'

'And about Count Nikolai's body,' I said.

'Something will be done,' said Magda. 'My father is seeing to it.'

At the bottom of the mountain road, where it

91

joined the larger highway, she turned the car to face the way we had come. 'Wait!' she said.

You could just see the broken outline of Castle Szekuli, black against the night sky.

A few minutes later there was a steady droning and a large shape came down out of the clouds. It swooped low over the castle. There was a series of rumbling thuds and the castle disappeared. A pillar of flame rose high into the sky as the jet-plane zoomed away.

Like his daughter, Colonel Roman believed in direct action.

'Wasn't that rather ruthless?' said Dad quietly. 'Those people were ill . . .'

'With an illness that still has no cure,' Magda reminded him. 'Would you have them live on as they are, Professor Stirling, drinking the blood of their family and friends, killing some and infecting others?'

Dad didn't reply.

Magda turned the car and we drove away.

Back in Bucharest Colonel Roman showered us with praise and thanks and bustled us on to the next available plane. He said the area around

Szekuli would be cordoned off and any surviving vampires rounded up. Work would begin at once to find a cure for the vampire disease.

All Dad's offers of help were politely refused. Romania wanted to deal with its own problems in its own way with absolutely no publicity – and no foreigners involved. Movie vampires were fine, but real ones were bad for the country's image.

Sergeant Janos drove us to the airport in the big black limousine and Colonel Roman and Magda came to see us off. As we stood waiting to board the plane, Magda turned to me and said, 'There is a message from the airport.'

'What is it?'

'It is a big field where aeroplanes land and take off!' She turned to her baffled father. 'This is an English joke.'

We said our goodbyes. Magda gave me a quick kiss on the lips and turned and disappeared into the limousine. I stood staring after her and Dad put a hand on my shoulder.

'Shall we get on the plane, Matthew, or will you fly home without it?'

As we settled into our seats I said, 'How much older can she be – three or four years? Five at the most. In a few years' time that won't matter at all . . .'

Dad fastened his seat belt. 'The sooner I get you home the better, Matthew. I prescribe lots of healthy exercise, regular cold showers – and no more late-night horror movies . . .'

That was the end of it – at least, I hope it was.

I never really made up my mind about Count Nikolai Szekuli.

Was he the madman Dad called him, or the super-vampire he claimed to be? Did he really have the power to ignore locked doors, to climb, bat-like, to a high locked window and somehow pass through?

Was his appearance in my room at the Hotel Magnifici real? Or was it imaginary, a phantom he'd planted in my mind with some hypnotic command?

Sometimes I remember what he said about living in London, and about having friends here, fellow exiles. Friends who might be vampires, perhaps? Who might want to avenge him?

I think about these things on dark and stormy nights when my bedroom curtains billow in the wind. I still keep the crucifix and the garlic handy in my bedside drawer.

After all, there's no point in taking unnecessary risks. You never know with vampires . . .

If you would like more information about
books available from Piccadilly Press and how
to order them, please contact us at:

Piccadilly Press Ltd.
5 Castle Road
London
NW1 8PR

Tel: 020 7267 4492
Fax: 020 7267 4493